"Billy's scared of the seagulls," I told Mrs Baines. "He won't come out. Not till they go away. Why are there so many?"

"They're waiting for the end of playtime, then they'll come down and gobble up the crumbs from all the snacks. Honestly, Billy," she said, "they won't eat children. Not without salt and vinegar anyway."

She should never have said that about eating children. Billy howled. He cried and cried and he wouldn't stop.

YOUNG CORGI BOOKS

Young Corgi books are perfect when you are looking for great books to read on your own. They are full of exciting stories and entertaining pictures. There are funny books, scary books, spine-tingling stories and mysterious ones. Whatever your interests you'll find something in Young Corgi to suit you: from ponies to football, from families to ghosts. The books are written by some of the most famous and popular of today's children's authors, and by some of the best new talents, too.

Whether you read one chapter a night, or devour the whole book in one sitting, you'll love Young Corgi books. The more you read, the more you'll want to read!

Also available by Paul May
Published by Corgi Pups for beginner readers:
CAT PATROL

Published by Young Corgi:
NICE ONE, SMITHY!

Published by Corgi Yearling for junior readers:
TROUBLEMAKERS
DEFENDERS
GREEN FINGERS
RAIN

Billy and the SEAGULLS

Paul May

Illustrated by Kate Sheppard

YOUNG CORGI

BILLY AND THE SEAGULLS
A YOUNG CORGI BOOK 9780552568746

Published in Great Britain by Corgi Books,
an imprint of Random House Children's Books

This edition published 2004

3 5 7 9 10 8 6 4 2

Young Corgi Books are published by Random ⋯ ⋯ooks,
61–63 Uxbridge Road, London W5 5SA,
a division of The Random House Group Ltd,
Addresses for companies within the Random House Group can be found at
www.randomhouse.co.uk/offices.htm

Printed and bound in Great Britain by Clays Ltd, St Ives plc

THE RANDOM HOUSE GROUP Limited Reg. No. 954009
www.kidsatrandomhouse.co.uk

A CIP catalogue record for this book is available from the British Library.

The Random House Group Limited supports The Forest Stewardship
Council® (FSC®), the leading international forest-certification organisation.
Our books carrying the FSC label are printed on FSC®-certified paper.
FSC is the only forest-certification scheme supported by the leading
environmental organisations, including Greenpeace. Our
paper procurement policy can be found at
www.randomhouse.co.uk/environment

MIX
Paper from
responsible sources
FSC® C018072

Contents

Contents

Chapter One

My Brother Billy

Nan said that our Billy was scared of his own shadow, but that wasn't quite true. It was just Nan's way of talking. In fact, it sometimes seemed like Billy's shadow was just about the only thing in the whole world that he *wasn't* scared of.

I reckon it was the earthquake that started it. It was just after our dad moved out, and Billy was only three. There was a programme on TV one night, with the earth shaking and people running out of their houses and buildings falling down.

"Sometimes," the man on TV said, "we even have earthquakes right here in Britain."

That did it. Billy hid behind the sofa. He didn't hear the man saying that British earthquakes were only tiny things that never hurt anyone. That was because he had his hands over his ears. Later that night me and Mum heard a wailing noise and there was

8

Billy, standing at the top of the stairs. He was shaking all over. "I'm w-w-w-w-worried about the earthquakes," he said, in a quivery voice, as if an earthquake was actually shaking him.

After that he started to worry about all sorts of things. There were all the usual ones, like snakes and spiders and darkness, but Billy was scared of daft things too, like toilets flushing, and Laurel and Hardy, and the skin on custard, and orange peel, and Lego, and men with moustaches . . .

I could go on. I made a list, but it's an incredibly long list, and you wouldn't believe me anyway. I mean, who's scared of *orange peel*?

Well, my brother Billy.

That's who.

Chapter Two

Soggy Toast

We were having our tea on Friday night. It was beans on toast again, but I didn't mind that. I liked beans on toast, and Billy liked them too. He usually shovelled them down, but tonight he was poking at his pile of beans with his fork and his hand was shaking.

"What is it now, Billy?" Mum said, with a big sigh. "What's the matter?"

"The toast," said Billy. He pointed at his plate, like he was looking at a ghost or a vampire or something. "It's all *soggy!*"

"It's always soggy," I told him. "It's the best bit. Here, have some of mine."

I speared a bit of soggy, tomatoey toast on my fork and waved it under his nose. Billy let out a howl you could have heard from the end of our street.

"Eddie!" yelled Mum.

That's me, by the way. Eddie Foster. You'd think Mum would have realized I was only trying to help. Now she was cross, I was fed up, and Billy had the shakes. It would have made a good film – *Nightmare at Teatime.*

That's when the front door opened and Dave walked in. He was singing. At least, I think it was *meant* to be

11

singing. We all stared at him. "Oh, I do like to be beside the seaside," he croaked, then he grabbed hold of Billy and whizzed him up into the air. "Well?" he asked us. "Who wants to go to the seaside?"

I'd better explain about Dave. Mum said he was our new dad, but we already had a dad, even if he didn't live with us any more, even if Mum and Dave *had* got married. Everyone liked Dave except me. Nan liked him. Billy liked him. And Mum liked him, obviously. I didn't *hate* him. I just didn't want a new dad, that was all.

Dave put Billy down. "Do it again," Billy yelled. He wasn't scared of heights. How weird is that?

"You're joking," I said to Dave. "Aren't you?"

"You got the job?" said Mum.

Dave just grinned at her. He grinned at all of us. Mum shrieked, threw her arms around him and kissed him.

"You mean it?" I said. "We can have a holiday?"

Dave looked at me. 'Not *exactly* a holiday," he said. "That's to say, it *is* the seaside. Definitely. We can go to the beach every day if we want to."

"What Dave is trying to tell you," said Mum, "is that his new job's in another town. A town by the sea. We're going to have to move."

Chapter Three

Hard Work

Billy and me had to go and stay with
Nan while Mum and Dave looked
for a house.

"Why can't we come with you?" I
asked. "We've got to live there too."

"Are you kidding?" said Dave.
"House-hunting with Billy? What if
we meet a man with a moustache?
What if there's soggy toast for breakfast? No thanks, Eddie."

So I stayed behind with Billy, and
that was hard work. Every night after
school I had to play with him and
look after him when he got the
shakes. The trouble was, you could
never tell when it was going to
happen. He found something new to
be scared of almost every day. He got

the shakes one night when he saw Nan with her hair in curlers. I had to put him to bed because Nan couldn't take the curlers out or she'd mess up her hair, and I had to read him six stories before he fell asleep. When he did, me and Nan sat on the bottom of his bed, watching him.

"Well," said Nan. "What a performance."

"You'll never be able to do your hair again when Billy's around," I said.

"He'll grow out of it," said Nan. "You mustn't worry about him. And you mustn't worry about moving either." She gave me a hug. Nan always knew what I was thinking without having to ask. "You'll soon make lots of new friends."

"I don't *want* to live anywhere else," I said. "It's not fair. And what about our dad? It'll be even further for him to come and see us. He'll *never* come."

At first when Dad left, he lived in the next town, and me and Billy sometimes went to visit him. Then he moved to Scotland, and now we didn't see him hardly at all. "Don't be daft," said Nan. "Everyone likes going to the seaside. You'll have plenty of visitors, you mark my words. It'll be a new start for all of you."

Mum and Dave came back the next day, all brown and smiling. "We've found a great place to live," Dave said. "You'll be able to see the sea from your bedroom window."

"I like *our* house," I said. "I like my school. I like my friends. Why can't you get a job *here*?"

Mum gave me one of her looks. "You wait till you see it," Dave said. "You'll change your mind pretty fast once you're there."

Chapter Four

Nothing To Be Afraid of

By the time moving day finally
arrived there was only a week of the
summer holidays left. You wouldn't
believe how long it takes to pack up
everything there is in a house,
especially with someone like Billy
helping.

We watched the van drive away with all our things. I just had time for a look inside the house before Mum slammed the front door for the last time. I'd lived there all my life, but now it didn't look like our home any more. It was all empty and sad.

I looked in the car, where me and Billy were supposed to sit. There was a box of food for a picnic, and about a million bags of all the stuff that wouldn't fit in the van. "We'll never get in there," I said.

"There's plenty of room," said Mum. There wasn't, but we had to get in anyway. Billy held his new bucket and spade and kept asking whether we were there yet, only we never were because it was hundred and hundreds of miles. I must have fallen asleep in the end, because Dave's voice woke me up. "Look!" he said. "Seagulls!"

There was a big sign at the side of the road saying, "Welcome to Eastleigh-on-Sea". Two enormous grey-and-white birds were perched on top of the sign. "Look, Billy," said Dave. "They're nearly as big as you are."

He'd stopped the car so we could see better. The gulls had long yellow beaks with big red spots near the end. They stared at us with their big yellow eyes. They looked *savage*. "Ben had this video," I said. "It was about a town where all the birds went crazy and started attacking people. They—"

"Eddie!" Mum hissed. "Shut up."

OK. I know it was stupid. I was half-asleep and I wasn't thinking properly, and if you ask me it was just as much Dave's fault for stopping the car. But it wasn't Dave who got the blame.

"I don't like them," said Billy, staring at the seagulls. I could see his bottom lip starting to tremble. "There's *blood* on their beaks."

"That's not blood," said Dave. He jumped out of the car. "They're just ordinary seagulls. Look."

He waved his arms at them, but they didn't move. They just stared right back at him. Dave took another step towards the gulls. They squawked once, then they flapped slowly into the air, as if they didn't really want to go. "See?" said Dave, getting back into the car. "Nothing to be afraid of."

"I don't like them," Billy said miserably. "I don't like it here. I want to go home."

Chapter Five

Sad

Our new house was a tall thin house in a street of tall thin houses. Billy's bedroom was in the attic, and when you looked out of his window you could sometimes see big ships going in and out of the harbour. Billy loved watching them. On our first Monday morning he didn't even want to come down for breakfast.

"Do you think he's all right?" asked Mum. "Maybe he's sickening for something."

"He's OK," said Dave, pulling on his jacket and trying to eat his toast at the same time. "At least it stops him worrying about the seagulls."

"While he's indoors," I said. "That's not much good, is it? We can't even go to the beach."

"And whose fault is that?" asked Mum, looking at me.

We'd tried going to the beach on Saturday, but it hadn't been any fun. There were seagulls *everywhere* in Eastleigh-on-Sea: on top of the lamp-posts, on the chimneys, and most of all on the beach. They hung around, waiting to snap up the crusts from people's sandwiches and the chips they didn't eat. I even saw one giant bird pulling empty fish and chip wrappers out of a rubbish bin. Billy sat on the beach with his hands over his eyes saying, "I don't like it here." We didn't stay long.

It was Dave's first day at work, and it was easy to see he was nervous. He'd already put the teapot in the fridge and lost the car keys three times. Mum straightened his tie and kissed him. "You'll be fine,' she said, and pushed him out of the door.

Later on Mum made us go into the town to buy new clothes for school. "Let's just hope there aren't too many you-know-whats," she said.

We couldn't even *mention* seagulls in front of Billy. I had to check the sky before we could go out of the front door, and we hadn't gone far before he spotted a couple of them perched on a chimney. He shut his eyes tight and wouldn't open them again until we got to the shops. But when he got his first ever school uniform on, he forgot all about seagulls.

"Cool!" he said, when he looked at himself in the mirror.

"No," I told him. "Sad."

"Shut up, Eddie," said Mum. "It's great that Billy wants to go to school. You should be pleased, because you're going to be looking after him, aren't you?"

And that was the trouble. I'd been worrying about it all summer. I mean, at home everyone *knew* about Billy. They thought he was funny. But at this new place – well, what would they think?

Chapter Six

What Big Ears You've Got

The school was full of sea things.
There were fishing nets and shells and
model boats in the entrance hall. You
could actually see the sea out of the
windows. The headteacher shook
hands with all of us, Billy included.

"I'm very pleased to meet you," she said. "My name is Mrs Baines. I . . ."

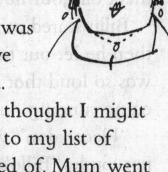

She stopped. Billy was staring at her. "You've got big ears," he said.

Just for a second I thought I might have to add big ears to my list of things Billy was scared of. Mum went bright red, and I tried not to laugh, because Mrs Baines *did* have big ears, but Mrs Baines just smiled.

"All the better to *hear* you with, my dear!" she said. I think it was meant to be a joke, but it was a bad mistake, because even if Billy wasn't scared of big ears, he was *definitely* scared of stories with wicked wolves in them. He started to shake, but Mrs Baines didn't notice. She smiled a pretend smile, like a wolf pretending to be a sweet little grandma. "Come along, Billy," she said, holding out a hand with bright red fingernails. "Let's go and meet all your new friends."

Billy stared at the fingernails, and then he let out this *enormous* howl. It was so loud that the school secretary came running out of her office.

"Please don't worry," said Mum nervously. "Billy's imagination runs away with him sometimes. It's your fingernails. He thinks they're . . ."

"Oh dear," said Mrs Baines, and she hid her hands behind her back.

"He'll be fine in a moment," said Mum. "He's dead keen to come to school. Aren't you, Billy?"

Billy nodded, but he wouldn't look at Mrs Baines. "I . . . I'll get Mrs Gooch to show you the way to Billy's classroom," Mrs Baines said. Her face had gone very pale. "I'll take Eddie to his class."

"See you later, Billy," I said. He toddled off along the corridor with Mum and Mrs Gooch. I started thinking about all the millions of things there would be in his classroom that might give him the shakes.

"Come along, Eddie," said Mrs Baines. "And don't look so worried. I'm sure your mum's right. Your little brother will settle in nicely."

Chapter Seven

Totally Nuts

When Mrs Baines opened the door of my new classroom there was rubbish everywhere. There were bottles, cans, newspapers and magazines. There were crisp packets, broken plates, old frying pans, radios, bits of car and rusty bicycle wheels. And in among the rubbish were the kids from Class Seven. They were wearing aprons and bright yellow gloves and safety goggles. They looked like weird sea creatures. They'd stopped whatever it was they were meant to be doing, and they were all looking at *me*.

A man with red overalls and untidy hair staggered out of a cupboard with an armful of magazines. "Aha!" he said. "Another pair of hands. Terrific.

You must be Eddie. I'm Mr Ingham."
He found a small space on the floor
and dumped the magazines. "We're
doing a project," he explained. "On
rubbish. Did you know, Eddie, that
just about everything here can be
recycled? And what do people do
with it? They dump it in big holes in
the ground, that's what."

Mum arrived while Mr Ingham
was talking. She gave me a thumbs-
up sign. "Isn't that a fantastic
coincidence?" she said to me. "Dave
could come in and tell everyone
about his job." She turned to Mr
Ingham and Mrs Baines. "Eddie's dad
works at a landfill site," she said.

That made me feel hot all over. I
couldn't help it. Everyone would be
staring at me. He's *not* my dad, I
thought. And why did he have to get
a job working in a *rubbish tip*? Why

did Mum have to tell everyone about
it anyway?

"Come on, Eddie," Mr Ingham
said. "You go and help Ruth and
Joseph over there. I'll just have a word
with your mum."

He gave me a pair of
goggles and some
gloves and an
apron. I'd only just
worked out how to
put them all on
when Mum was
back. "I'm off now,"
she said, kissing me.
Anyone would have
thought she was
actually *trying* to embarrass me.
"Have a good day. And you won't
forget about Billy, will you?"

As if I could.

"Who's Billy?" asked Ruth.

"My little brother," I told her. "He's just started in Class One."

"Yeah?" Ruth lifted her goggles up and there were a pair of glasses and big green eyes. "My little brother started today too. I hope I don't have to look after *him*."

"Why not?"

"Are you kidding?" she said. "He's totally nuts."

"Ruth's right." The creature next to Ruth lifted his goggles. He grinned.

He didn't have any of his front teeth. "I'm Joseph," he said. "My little sister Sarah, she's nuts too. All little kids are the same." He chucked a lemonade bottle into a big green bin, and I started to feel a tiny bit better. Maybe they were right, I told myself. Maybe Billy wasn't any different from the rest of them. Maybe he'd be fine.

I was still thinking that when play-time arrived.

Chapter Eight

Snack Attack

"Haven't you got a snack?" Joseph
asked me, opening a packet of crisps.
"Here, have some of mine."

He held out the packet just as we
were going through the door.
Something swooped past, right over
our heads. I ducked, and Joseph
laughed. "It's only the seagulls," he
said. "They come every day."

The sky was full of birds, all
swirling around and shrieking. They

dived down in between people and screamed up into the sky again. There were hundreds of them.

"I've got to find my brother," I said. "He's got spiky brown hair and a red T-shirt. He must be somewhere."

A little girl came charging up to us and threw her arms around Joseph. He looked embarrassed and tried to prise her off. "My sister, Sarah," he said sheepishly. "Totally nuts."

"No, you are," said his sister.

"Have you seen my brother?" I asked her. "He's called Billy."

"Billy's funny," Sarah said. "He's hiding." She pointed to a flowerbed. "He went in there."

I pushed between the bushes and there was Billy, right in the middle. His eyes were shut tight, he had his hands over his ears *and* he was shaking. "It's OK, Billy," I told him.

"I'll take you inside."

"I c-c-c-c-c-c-can't." Billy was shaking so much his teeth were chattering. I heard footsteps coming through the bushes. I heard Mrs Baines's voice, sounding very cross, saying, "Come out of there at once." Then she saw us. "Oh," she said. "Eddie. And Billy. Whatever are you doing?"

"Billy's scared of the seagulls," I told her. "He won't come out. Not till they go away. Why are there so many?"

"They're waiting for the end of play-time, then they'll come down and gobble up the crumbs from all the snacks. Honestly, Billy," she said, "they won't eat children. Not without salt and vinegar anyway."

She should never have said that about eating children. Billy howled. He cried and cried and he wouldn't stop. Then the bell went and I heard everybody starting to go back into school.

The seagulls were going crazy. They were swooping right over the heads of the children, diving down to pick up crisps, pecking and screaming. Then suddenly they were gone, just white specks, way out over the sea.

Billy was very pale and quiet. "It's safe now," I told him, "They've all gone."

"Are you sure?" said Billy.

"Sure," I said. I held out my hand and Billy took it.

"Does this sort of thing happen very often, Eddie?" Mrs Baines asked me. I noticed she'd taken off the red nail varnish, so at least she had *some* sense.

"Well . . . sort of," I said. We'd arrived at Billy's classroom and he ran straight off to play in the sandpit with Sarah. He was smiling. It was like the sun coming out after a thunderstorm.

Mrs Baines watched him go. "I expect he'll soon get used to the seagulls," she said hopefully.

I thought about my list. I'd never ever crossed anything off it. I shook my head. "I don't think he will," I said.

"Well then," said Mrs Baines, "in that case, we really have no choice. The seagulls will just have to get their snacks somewhere else."

Chapter Nine

Starvation

We had assembly after lunch – the whole school together in the hall. "Some of the children in Mrs Jackson's class are getting upset about the seagulls," Mrs Baines said. "And they *can* be rather scary if you're not used to them. So I've decided that we'll stop having snacks at playtimes."

Everyone groaned. "But we'll starve," said Barry. I knew his name because Mr Ingham had already told him off about a hundred times that morning.

"Nonsense, Barry," said Mrs Baines. "You'll work up an appetite for your dinner, that's all."

"It's not fair," said Ruth afterwards. "Just because one little kid is scared of seagulls."

"Billy can't help it," I said. "He's never seen seagulls before. You all grew up here so it's all right for you."

"No one's scared of *seagulls*," Barry said. "You should tell him not to be so daft."

They were all looking at me. I could see they all agreed. But then I heard a voice beside me. "I never liked them when I started school," Joseph said. "I used to cry. I can remember. And so did you, Ruth."

Ruth went bright red. "I was only a *little* bit scared," she said. "And anyway, I wasn't the only one."

"So what?" said Barry. "None of us went bonkers, did we? Mrs Baines never had to ban snacks because of *us*."

I nearly thumped him, only Joseph stopped me, and then Mr Ingham came in and we had to start on the rubbish again.

At home time all the mums and dads were waiting in the playground. I heard a little girl next to me say, "We can't have snacks any more, Mum. It's not fair. It's because of that boy there."

She pointed. They were all looking in the same direction, all the mums and dads and all the children. Billy was standing in the doorway, holding Mrs Jackson's hand. His eyes were shut tight.

"Mrs Foster?" Mrs Jackson said to Mum. "I wonder if I could talk to you for a moment?"

"I knew it," Mum sighed.

"I couldn't help it," I told her. "There were seagulls everywhere."

"It's not just the seagulls, I'm afraid," said Mrs Jackson. "There's the toilets, and the Lego and . . ."

"Come on," said Mum. "We'd better go inside."

Chapter Ten

HOW COULD YOU?

When we got home, Billy went straight up to his room to watch the boats.

"How about you, Eddie?" Mum asked me. "Did you make any friends today?"

"Yeah, right," I said. "My little brother forces everyone to starve at playtimes and I'm supposed to have *friends*."

"Oh, come on, Eddie, I'm sure no one blames you. I bet those seagulls will just clear off as soon as they realize there's nothing to eat, and you heard what Mrs Jackson said – lots of children find it difficult, starting school. Billy will soon settle down."

"Huh!" I said. Then the door opened and Dave came in, grinning all over his face.

"Guess what?" he said. "I don't just work in the office. I get to try *everything*. They're even going to let me drive this *enormous* digger. When I've finished my training I'll be a fully qualified Landfill Technician and . . ."

I stopped listened. I was fed up
with everything. And I was especially
fed up with Dave for making us come
here. I went upstairs and there was
Billy, staring out of the window while
he chewed the chocolate off a biscuit
as if there was nothing wrong in the
whole world. A huge blue ship was
moving slowly through the harbour.
Gulls were circling behind it.

"Look, Billy," I said. "They're not hurting anyone, are they? Seagulls don't hurt *people*, so there's no point being scared of them, is there?"

Billy put his hands over his ears. I thought about what Joseph had said. He'd been scared of the seagulls at first, but he'd got used to them. Maybe if I showed Billy some pictures . . .

I ran to my room and pulled books out of one of the boxes until I found my big bird book. "Look!" I said. I shoved a picture of herring gulls under Billy's nose. "They're just *birds*, Billy. They can't hurt you. They—"

Mum came rushing into the room. She was *very* angry. "What are you doing, Eddie?" she yelled. "How *could* you?"

Billy was trembling. I saw the tears running down his cheeks and I felt terrible. "I didn't *mean* to—" I began.

"That's the trouble," Mum said. "You never do."

Chapter Eleven

I Want To Go Home

I went to my bedroom. I heard Mum go downstairs and then, after a little while, she came back up again and opened my door. "Here," she said, handing me the phone. "Your dad wants a word."

"Eddie?" Dad's voice was tiny and crackly. "How are you doing? How's the new house? How's the new school?"

"When are you coming to see us, Dad?" I said. "You are going to come, aren't you?"

"You know it's difficult," Dad said. "What with the new baby and everything."

I didn't tell you about the new baby, did I? It wasn't just Mum who'd

got married again. Dad had too. He
had a wife called Ellen and now
there was this baby called Jamie.
Another little brother.

"Are you still there, Eddie?" Dad
asked. "Tell me about Billy. What's he
been up to now?"

So I told Dad about the seagulls.
"Listen," he said, when I'd finished.

"It's bound to be tough at first, but things'll get better. And I'm going to come and visit as soon as I can. You can meet your new baby brother. That's something to look forward to, isn't it?"

I switched off the phone and went into Billy's room. Dave was sitting on Billy's bed, reading him a story. Billy had stopped shaking. He was laughing and Dave was laughing too.

Billy liked Dave. It didn't bother Billy that Dave wasn't our real dad – and sometimes he actually forgot and called Dave *Dad*.

I hated that.

But I'll tell you something else. I knew that what Mum would really, really like, more than almost anything else, would be if I'd call Dave *Dad*, just the way Billy did. You wouldn't think one little word could matter so much, would you?

But every time I thought about saying it I felt wobbly inside. And I did think about it. I thought about it every day.

Seagull Protection

The next morning, Billy wouldn't get up. When Mum tried to make him, he grabbed hold of the mattress and wouldn't let go. "I'm not going to school," he kept saying, over and over. "I'm not, *I'm not*, I'M NOT."

Then Dave came in. "Leave this to me," he said.

So me and Mum went downstairs. I was on my third spoonful of Chocolate Crunchies when Dave and Billy came in.

"You'll be late," Mum said to Dave.

"It doesn't matter," said Dave. "I'm taking the boys to school. Special seagull protection squad. Got to make sure Billy gets there safely. Right, Billy?"

Billy dipped a finger of toast into his boiled egg and pulled it out again, all dripping yellow. It was disgusting. Why wasn't he scared of *that*? "Dad's going to hold the umbrella," Billy said. "So I don't see the seagulls."

"An umbrella!" I said. "We'll look stupid. Everyone will laugh at us. They already think Billy's bonkers."

"Eddie!" said Mum. Dave looked at me and I saw that his eyes were angry too, and Dave was *never* angry.

Billy looked up from his egg. "What does bonkers mean?" he said.

"Nothing," said Dave. "Nothing at all."

I knew I shouldn't have said it. There was a moment's silence, then Mum said: "Well, I think Dave's idea is great." She looked at me, daring me to argue.

So there was Dave in his orange overalls holding a huge stripy umbrella on a bright sunny day, and Billy skipping along underneath holding Dave's hand. I tried to pretend I wasn't with them, but when we got to school, Joseph saw me straight away. Loads of people were laughing at Billy.

"Is that your dad?" Joseph asked me.

Dave was talking to Mrs Baines. They were laughing about the umbrella. Dave waved to me.

"He *is* your dad, isn't he?" Joseph said. "He looks cool. He—"

"He's called Dave," I said. "He's not my *real* dad, OK? And it's none of your business anyway."

Joseph looked at me. "All right, then," he said. "Be like that. See if I care."

Chapter Thirteen

The Birds

The seagulls came back at playtime.
They swooped around at first, then
some of them started to settle down
on the edge of the school roof. Billy's
class didn't even come outside. Mrs
Jackson didn't let them. It was creepy,
all those birds sitting up there. After a
while, the playground went quiet.
"You know what?" I heard Joseph
say. "I think they're angry."

"You mean hungry," said Ruth, glancing over at me. I couldn't tell if she was joking or not. "Like us."

"Right," said Barry. He looked at me too. "Hungry *and* angry. They want their snacks."

I stood up. "It's not my fault," I began. "You can't blame me."

"What is going on?" said Mr Ingham. He'd come out to ring the bell. He looked up and saw the gulls.

"It's weird," said Joseph.

"My dad's got this film," said Barry. "It's called *The Birds*. The birds in this town all go crazy and start attacking people, and then . . ."

I looked at Barry. "That's what I thought—" I began, but Mr Ingham interrupted. "Enough," he said. "These birds will clear off as soon as they realize you lot aren't chucking half a ton of crisps on the playground every day. You wait and see."

So we did wait, and Mr Ingham was wrong. Every day it got more like the film. More and more birds came and sat on the roof. Every day Billy came to school with his umbrella. The idea caught on, and by the end of the week loads of the little kids were bringing umbrellas to school, but they still couldn't go out to play.

In Class Seven we sorted rubbish and drew pictures of rubbish. We made graphs about rubbish, and we wrote about it. Everyone was supposed to be collecting rubbish and taking it into school so we could sort it and recycle it. We were trying to tidy up a bit one afternoon when Barry turned and said, "Hey, look at me!"

He had his goggles and his overalls on, but he also had an old yellow lampshade on his head, and he was holding a plastic bottle over each ear and waggling the fingers of his extra large yellow rubber gloves. That's when I had the brilliant idea. It was like a lightbulb switching on in my head.

"I've got it!" I said.

"What?" said Barry and Joseph together.

"We could make scarecrows," I said. "It's obvious. We could use all this stuff. We could make a hundred scarecrows with what we've got here. We can scare the seagulls away, and they'll never come back."

Chapter Fourteen

Vampire

At my last school I'd
always had good ideas.
I was famous for them.
But this was the first one
I'd had for a long time.

"He'll never let us do
it," Barry said.

"But it *is* a good
idea," said Joseph, and gave
me a toothless grin. As soon as Mr
Ingham arrived I asked him.

"I don't know, Eddie," he said when
I'd explained. "We're supposed to be
taking all this stuff to the recycling
centre on Friday. We have to do
literacy and numeracy as well, you
know."

"But Mr Ingham," Ruth said,

"building scarecrows would be technology, wouldn't it? And art, if we make artistic scarecrows. And science, too, because we'll be trying to find out what seagulls are scared of."

I looked at Ruth. There were brains behind those glasses. "It would be literacy, too," I said, "if we wrote about it. And . . ."

"Well, maybe," Mr Ingham scratched his head. "But I don't know what Mrs Baines would say."

"It can be a surprise," Joseph said. "Mrs Baines will be really pleased. She says Mrs Jackson will go crazy if the little ones don't go out to play soon. We'll all be heroes. And heroines," he added, looking at Ruth.

Mr Ingham looked around the room. We all sat there like statues, waiting.

"OK," he said finally. "We'll do it."

It took days to make the scarecrows. I made mine with Barry and Joseph.

"It's got to be really scary," Barry said.

"We could make it look like Mrs Baines," said Joseph.

"But the gulls aren't scared of her," I said. "Why don't we make a vampire? Everyone knows vampire films are the scariest."

"That's brilliant," said Barry. "We'll give it a white face."

"And dripping fangs," said Joseph.

"And a long black cloak that flaps in the wind," I said. "Look. We can use rubbish bags."

So we got cardboard boxes and lemonade bottles and rolled-up news-paper to make the body and the arms, then we stuck it all together with brown sticky tape and gave it an enormous head with staring eyes and straggly hair made out of wire and string. It was the scariest scarecrow of all. Everyone said so.

I just *knew* it was going to work.

Chapter Fifteen

Too Late

We made invitations on the computer for all the other classes and teachers.

GRAND SEAGULL SCARING
FRIDAY MORNING PLAY
COME AND SEE CLASS SEVEN
SCARE ALL THE SEAGULLS AWAY
(FOR GOOD)

"See?" said Barry, when we'd printed it out and showed Mr Ingham. "It's poetry."

"Hmm," said Mr Ingham. "Go on, then. You'd better deliver them, then we'll get the scarecrows outside."

We carried all the scarecrows out onto the playground. They looked amazing. Some of them were like ordinary people, but some were gigantic monsters, like the one Ruth and her friends made. And then there was our vampire.

The tattered cloak fluttered in the wind and the black hair flipped up and down. It looked like it might take off at any moment and fly across the playground. If I'd been a seagull I would have been terrified. Then the doors opened and everyone came out to play.

I should have known what would happen. It was all right at first. Everyone was impressed, even the big kids in the top class. But the seagulls

didn't move, and slowly everyone went quiet. Barry charged at them suddenly, waving his arms. "Go away!" he yelled. "Leave us alone."

That's when I saw someone pushing through the crowd by the door. It was Mrs Jackson. "Have they gone?" she said. "What marvellous scarecrows!" Then she looked up and saw the seagulls. "Children!" she shouted. "Stop! Wait!"

STOP! WAIT!

But it was no good. All those little kids hadn't been out to play for days. They came bouncing out of the door like ping-pong balls. There was Sarah, and Ruth's brother, Darren, and then there was Billy. He took two steps onto the playground, and then he saw our vampire. He froze. He looked slowly around the playground and his eyes got wider and wider. Just for a second I thought it would be all right, but an extra strong gust of wind caught the vampire's black cloak and lifted it into the air. Billy started to shake. One seagull flapped up into the air. It squawked once and then glided down and settled right on the top of the vampire's head.

I started running towards Billy, but I knew it was too late.

Billy ran indoors, screaming.

Chapter Sixteen

The List

"Really, Eddie," Mum said when we got home. "How could you be so stupid?"

"I was trying to make it better," I said. "I was trying to *help*."

"Oh, Eddie," Mum said. "Billy was just starting to settle down. He'd gone a whole week without getting the shakes, and look at him now."

"It wouldn't have made any difference what our scarecrows were like," I said. "Billy's scared of soggy toast."

Billy was sitting on the bottom of the stairs. "I'm not," he said.

"Not what?"

"I'm not scared of soggy toast," Billy said. "Not any more. I had it at Sarah's house last night. It was nice."

I don't know why, but that made me more fed up than ever. I went upstairs to my room, and there on my noticeboard was the list. There were three pages. The last thing on the list was SEAGULLS. The very first thing, in quite babyish writing, was EARTH-QUAKES. SOGGY TOAST was near the end of the last page, just before NAN'S CURLERS.

I got a pencil and crossed it out. That's when Billy came in.

"What's that?" he said.

"It's my list of all the things you're scared of," I told him. "I've just crossed out SOGGY TOAST. Look."

"I can't *help* being scared of seagulls," Billy said. "I thought the scarecrows were cool. Sarah did too. Except . . ."

"Except the vampire," I said.

Billy nodded. Then he said: "What other things don't I like?"

"Lots and lots."

"Tell me. Maybe I'm not scared of some of them any more." He pointed. "What does that say?"

"Laurel and Hardy."

"Oh." Billy shivered a little. "What about that one?"

"Men with moustaches."

Billy shivered again and he looked up at me. His eyes were very blue. Then he pointed to the list again.

"What's that one?" he said.

"Wicked wolves."

Billy thought about that for a minute. Then he went and pulled my special book of fairy stories off the shelf, the one with the really scary pictures. He opened the book and turned the pages very carefully until he came to the story of *Little Red Riding Hood*. "Read this," he said.

"Are you sure?" I asked him. I knew what he was doing. He was trying to be brave. The trouble was, what would most likely happen was Billy would get the shakes, and I'd be in trouble all over again. But Billy was already looking at the first picture, snuggling up beside me. "Go on," he said.

Oh, well, I thought, it can't possibly make it any worse.

So I started to read.

Chapter Seventeen

Little Red Riding Hood

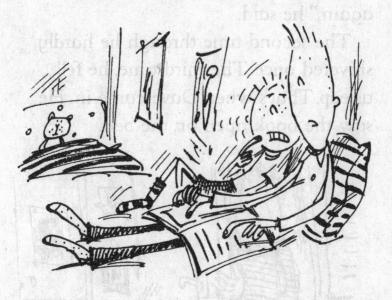

Billy held my hand, and when Red
Riding Hood met the wolf in the
forest he squeezed it hard, and kept
on squeezing. When I got to the bit
about "What big ears you have . . ."
Billy started to shake, just a tiny bit.
"D-d-d-don't stop," he said. "Read
about the eyes . . . and the t-t-t-eeth."

So I read about the eyes and the
teeth. When I'd finished, Billy was
pale, and his eyes were wide. "Read it
again," he said.

The second time through he hardly
shivered once. The third time, he fell
asleep. That's when Dave came in. He
saw the book open on the bed.

"You're not reading him that?" he said. I thought he was going to be cross, but he wasn't.

"It was Billy's idea," I told him. "I think he's trying to make himself braver."

Dave laughed quietly. "He's a funny kid, isn't he?" he said, and he stroked Billy's hair, just the way Nan stroked mine sometimes. After a moment he lifted Billy up very gently and carried him into his room. He tucked Billy into his bed, then he gave him a kiss on the top of his head and tiptoed out of the room. "I wanted to talk to you, Eddie," he said.

"It wasn't my fault," I said. "Mum always thinks it's my fault when Billy gets scared of things, but it's not. It's not fair."

"I know," said Dave.

"And Mum knew we were making

scarecrows. She—" I stopped. "What did you say?"

"I think the scarecrows were a great idea," Dave said.

"Even the vampire?"

Dave laughed. "I'd like to see it sometime," he said.

"It might be useful for scaring little kids," I said. "But it didn't scare the seagulls."

"That's what I wanted to tell you," said Dave. "I think I've found out how to get rid of them. There's something I want to show you. We can go tomorrow if you like. Just you and me. How about it?"

You probably think it's strange, but even though Mum had been going out with Dave for two years before they got married, and they'd been married nearly a year, so that makes three whole years, in all that time I'd never once been out with Dave on my own.

"OK," I heard myself say.

Dave messed up my hair and then went downstairs, singing to himself. It was a horrible noise, but somehow I didn't mind.

Chapter Eighteen

Goosebumps

"Hey, Billy," said Dave the next morning, when we were having our breakfast. "Eddie reckons you're not scared of wicked wolves any more."

Billy didn't say anything, but he smiled a sort of secret smile. "How about seagulls?" Dave asked him. "You still worried about them?"

Billy stopped chewing and thought very hard for about thirty seconds. Then he nodded and started chewing again.

"Let's go then, Eddie," Dave said. "You can finish that toast in the car."

"Where are you going?" said Billy. "What about me?"

I looked at my little brother. I knew Dave wanted it to be just me and him, but it wasn't any fun being left at home when other people were out having a good time. I knew all about that. "It's OK, Billy," I told him. "You can come too."

We drove out into the countryside. We passed tractors ploughing the fields, turning them from gold to brown. The earth looked like chocolate, and every tractor we saw had a flock of seagulls swirling behind it. The funny thing was, Billy didn't seem to mind.

"What are they doing?" he asked.

"Eating worms," said Dave. "They're always looking for an easy meal. The tractor does the work and the seagulls pick up the worms. Just like they eat the crumbs from your snacks. Just like . . . well, you'll see. Look, we've arrived."

Dave turned down a narrow lane and I saw the sign. LANDFILL SITE. At the end of the lane there were some sheds that looked a bit like the mobile classrooms we used to have at my old school, and a sandy path leading up a hill. "Come on," said Dave. "Follow me."

I held Billy's hand. We walked up the path and suddenly we were standing at the edge of an enormous cliff. Way down below three yellow diggers were parked. They looked like toys. "Wow!" said Billy. He didn't seem to be scared of looking over the edge of the cliff, which was strange, because it made me feel dizzy, and my insides felt a bit weird and I started to wish I hadn't eaten quite so much breakfast. I stepped back from the edge. I couldn't understand how Billy could just look down like that.

"Here we are," said Dave. "Come and meet Mr Cobbold."

Billy tugged at my arm, and we followed Dave along the path. An old man was standing there. He had a big leather glove on one hand. His face was dark brown and wrinkled from being outside all the time and he smiled when he saw us. Then he began to swing something around his head on the end of a piece of string, and he called some words into the sky.

"Look!" whispered Dave. "Up there." My eyes followed his pointing finger into the blue sky. There was a tiny black dot, high above us. "It's a falcon," said Dave. "A peregrine falcon. All the other birds are scared of it. Watch."

Mr Cobbold called again. And then the falcon dived.

It was almost too fast to see, and suddenly I knew I couldn't watch. I closed my eyes, and shivered. When I opened them again Mr Cobbold was smiling at us, beckoning us over. "Come on, boys," he said. "Come and meet my pretty little Sal."

The bird was perched on his hand. It was tearing at a lump of meat with its hooked beak. Its yellow claws were clamped onto the man's leather glove. The strangest thing was happening to me. I'd gone all cold. There were goosebumps on my arms and my hands had started to tremble. "I c-c-c-c-can't," I said. I knew what was happening to me. There was no doubt about it.

I had the shakes.

Chapter Nineteen

Two Hundred Miles An Hour

I felt Dave's arm around my shoulders. "It's OK, Eddie," he said. "You'll be all right in a sec."

"I'm sorry," I said. "I can't help it." I looked at the bird. You would never have guessed it could streak out of the sky like that. "Can it really scare seagulls away?" I asked Dave. I didn't really need to ask. I could see why the seagulls would be scared.

"You see any seagulls around here?" Dave asked me. "They come after the rubbish, just like they come after your snacks at school. But not when that little bird's in the sky." Then he stopped. "Look!" he whispered. "Look at Billy."

Billy was edging towards the old man. His hands were shaking, and he was going very slowly, watching the bird all the time.

"Billy!" I called. "What are you doing?"

"I want to see the bird."

Billy was right next to Mr Cobbold now. The old man smiled at him. "No need to be afraid of her," he said. "She's used to children. Would you like to hold her?"

Billy nodded and held out his hand. It made me feel strange, just watching him. Mr Cobbold pulled another glove from his bag, just like the one he was wearing. "Here," he said. "You put this on."

Dave bent down and helped Billy with the glove. Then Mr Cobbold squatted down and let the bird hop onto Billy's arm. There were pieces of leather trailing from the bird's legs, and bells rang when she moved.

"That's the way," said Mr Cobbold.

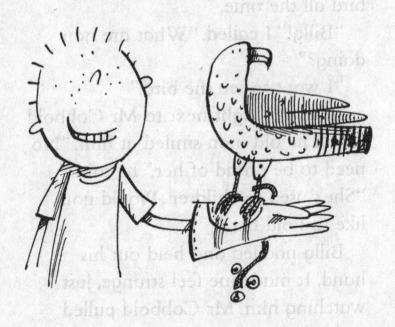

"You hold the jesses like this." He wound the leather between Billy's fingers. "There," he said. "Now she can't fly until you want her to."

"I want her to fly," Billy said. "I do."

He was staring right into the falcon's eyes and he wasn't shaking one little bit. "You mustn't stare," Mr Cobbold said. "She'll think you're an enemy."

Bill looked at Mr Cobbold instead. Mr Cobbold smiled at him. "Lift your arm. That's it. Now let her slip."

"Oh!" said Billy. The falcon flew away like an arrow, then she circled up until she was just a tiny dot. Mr Cobbold took the glove from Billy, but he hardly noticed. He was too busy gazing up into the sky.

"How do the seagulls know?" I said. "She looks so small."

"They're clever beggars," Mr Cobbold grunted. "You've seen how fast she comes down. She could knock one of them straight out of the sky if she wanted, before they even knew what had hit 'em. Not that I'd let her," he added, looking at Billy. "Those seagulls think she wants to kill them and eat them. If I let her kill one, they'd reckon she wasn't hungry any more, see? So they'd all come back."

He took the piece of string from his bag and he fastened a piece of meat to the end of it and he called. "Sal! Sal!"

I shut my eyes. I heard a voice saying, "Dad."

Then I realized it was *my* voice. I felt Dave's big hand holding mine. I felt stupid, but really glad at the same time. And suddenly I knew that even

if I *had* got one dad already, that
didn't mean I couldn't have another
one.

"Are you all right now?" Dave
asked me.

"Yeah," I said. I opened my eyes,
and I saw that Billy was watching us.
"I'm fine."

Chapter Twenty

Two Dads

When we got home a shiny red car was parked outside our house.

The front door opened and there was Dad, with a little baby in his arms. "Hi, Eddie," said Dad. "Hi, Billy. Come and meet your new baby brother. This is Jamie."

I got out of the car, but Billy was quicker. He rushed past me and started trying to look at the baby and tell Dad about Sal and the seagulls and the scarecrows, only it was all muddled up and didn't make any sense at all. Dad and Dave both started laughing and Mum came out of the door with Dad's wife, Ellen, and they started laughing too. Then Nan appeared. "Well," she said. "This *is* a party and no mistake."

It was a warm, sunny day with fluffy white clouds floating in the sky. After a while Dad said, "When shall we go to the beach?" and everyone went quiet.

"Sorry," he said quickly. "I forgot. The seagulls."

"You go," said Dave. "It would be daft not to on a day like this."

Billy stood up. "I want to come," he said. "I'm not scared of seagulls. Not any more."

When we got to the beach Joseph and his little sister Sarah were there, making a big sandcastle with their mum. There were seagulls floating around above people's heads, just waiting for a chance to swoop down and grab some food. Billy gave them one quick look, and then ran off down to the sea with Sarah to collect water in her bucket.

"What have you done to him?" said Mum to me and Dave. "He was a quivering jelly yesterday. Now look at him."

"Nothing," I said. "He did it all himself."

"Come on," said Dave. "Let's play cricket."

So me and Joseph played cricket with Dad and Dave, and I got all mixed up and kept calling Dad Dave and Dave Dad, until I could hardly remember which was which and it didn't really seem to matter any more. In the end Dave and Dad walked off together to where Mum and Ellen were sunbathing.

"So, actually," Joseph said to me, "you've got *two* dads."

"Yeah," I said. I felt very happy. "I suppose I have."

That's when I saw the seagull. It was huge, the biggest one I'd ever seen, and it was tugging at a plastic bag full of sandwiches, trying to pull it out of our picnic basket. I yelled, but Billy had already seen it. He was walking towards it with his spade in his hand.

As Billy took a step forward, the seagull gave one more tug at the bag, then it lifted its head and stared Billy in the eye. Billy stared back. Then he took one more step, and the seagull gave a loud shriek and flapped its wings. It circled around above us, shrieking angrily, but we were all laughing and cheering.

"Now we know how to get rid of the seagulls at school," said Joseph. "Billy can scare them away."

I looked at him. "Well, actually . . ." I said.

And I told him what was going to happen on Monday morning.

Chapter Twenty-one

Just In Time

It was nearly playtime, and the playground was full of people. All the teachers were there, and all the dinner ladies and cooks. There were lots of mums and dads there too, because Joseph's mum had told absolutely everyone, including the local paper. A reporter was talking to Mrs Baines and a photographer was busy taking snaps of the seagulls. They were sitting on every bit of the roof, and more of them were swooping around over our heads. Their shadows made patterns on the playground.

I looked for Mum and Dave. They were standing at the edge of the crowd. Dad and Ellen were there too, and Nan, holding up my new baby brother. They were all watching Billy.

The children in Billy's class were right at the front. They were staring at Sal; she was perched on Mr Cobbold's arm with her hood over her head. "Sal's going to scare the

102

seagulls away," Billy told them. He said it in a big, loud voice. Mum had spent ages in the morning spiking his hair up with gel until it looked like an extra prickly hedgehog. That's my little brother, I thought. I could hardly believe it.

Up on the roof the seagulls waited. None of them moved. They didn't seem to be worried about Sal at all, and a horrible thought came into my head. What if it all went wrong? What if they were a special kind of super-intelligent seagull that wasn't scared of falcons?

Mrs Jackson was thinking the same thing. "Look at them," she said to Mr Cobbold. "They're not afraid of her. They don't seem to be afraid of any-thing."

"They're clever, that's why," Mr Cobbold said. "They know she can't hurt them, not when she's sitting here." Billy was right beside him. He was looking up at the seagulls. Just for a second I thought his eyes looked a bit like Sal's.

Mr Cobbold hadn't moved. He was watching the seagulls too. "I reckon we're only just in time," he said. "They think that roof's a cliff. They think that's a good place to live. They'll start nesting up there when the spring comes, if we don't shift them. Are you ready?" he asked Billy.

Billy nodded. He held Mr Cobbold's hand and they walked off together towards the middle of the playground. Mr Cobbold loosened Sal's hood and took it off. Sal hopped onto Billy's arm. The photographer took his picture.

"Wow!" said Joseph. "Billy is so cool."

"You know what?" said Barry. He was standing right beside me. "We never had half this much fun before you and Billy came here."

I felt so proud I thought I would burst. I looked over to where Mum and Dave were standing. Dad and Ellen were standing a little behind them. Dad was watching Billy. I knew he was proud like me, but he looked sad, too. I waved to him and he smiled, but I knew he was thinking how he missed us. Just like I missed him.

Chapter Twenty-two

The Ginger Moustache

Billy was standing on his own now, with Sal on his arm. He looked so small. Then he lifted his hand, and Sal flew. Her wings beat quickly as she climbed into the sky, and I felt my heart beating fast inside my chest.

Everyone went very quiet. There was a long, long silence then, suddenly, all the seagulls lifted into the air. They drifted higher and higher, all together in a big crowd, following Sal as she circled up. Just then the sun came out from behind a cloud and dazzled me so that I had to shut my eyes.

When I opened them again the sky was empty except for one black dot high above. The seagulls had scattered and gone.

And then I heard Billy's voice, calling. "Sal!" he called. "Hey, Sal!" Mr Cobbold was swinging the lure around his head. I felt the hairs standing up on the back of my neck. I felt that strange trembling starting up inside me, but I wasn't scared any more. I was excited. I could feel it rushing through me like a river. I was excited about *everything*, my new school, Billy growing up, Mum and Dave, Dad and Ellen, my new baby brother. I looked at the faces of my new friends gazing up into the sky and I *wanted* to watch Sal dive. I didn't want to miss a second.

Then she came, at two hundred miles an hour. If that little bit of meat Mr Cobbold was swinging round his head had been a seagull, it would have had no chance.

Sal sat on the grass at Mr Cobbold's feet, tearing at her food, and everyone clapped and cheered. And they clapped and cheered even more a few minutes later when the cooks brought out big trays full of biscuits and cakes and drinks.

"Luckily for us," Mrs Baines announced, "Mr Cobbold is retiring from his job at the landfill site. Starting next week he's going to come to our school every day and fly Sal. So from now on, we can all have our playtime snacks again."

Mr Cobbold grinned. "Lovely cakes," he said, licking crumbs from his lips. "Do you have these every day?"

Mrs Baines laughed. "I'm sure we can arrange something," she told him. "Now everyone, tuck in. But don't leave any crumbs. There are no seagulls to pick them up for you."

It was like a big party, but it was over much too soon, and Nan and Dad and Ellen had to go. Dad hugged me. "Ring me any time," he said. "Not just when you're in trouble, eh?"

"OK," I said. Dad picked Billy up and gave him a big hug too, then they all got in the car and drove away. Me and Billy kept on waving until the car turned the corner.

"Come on," said Dave, smiling. "That reporter wants to talk to you both." I held Billy's hand and we walked over to where the photographer was taking a picture of Mrs Baines and Mr Cobbold.

The photographer turned round. "Aha!" he said to Billy. "The hero of the hour. And you must be his brother. Eddie, isn't it? I've been hearing about a vampire scarecrow. Any chance of a picture of you and your vampire? And the other scare-crows too. It's going to make a terrific story, is this."

"Oh," said Mum. "I don't think that's such a good idea. Maybe later . . ."

But Billy said, "I'm not scared of vampires any more. Or scarecrows. Me and Sarah went and looked at them. They aren't real, you know."

"Oh, right," said Mum. "Of course not. Silly me."

Then the reporter arrived. "OK, then," he said. "Eddie Foster, is it? And Billy?"

"Yes," I said. But Billy didn't say anything. He was staring up at the reporter's face. There, right under-neath the reporter's big red nose, was a bristly ginger moustache.

Billy's bottom lip started to tremble.

His hands started to shake.

He began to howl . . .

THE END